Freight Train
Donald Crews

 Greenwillow Books

Freight Train. Copyright © 1978 by Donald Crews. All rights reserved. Manufactured in China.
For information address HarperCollins Children's Books, a division of HarperCollins Publishers, 195 Broadway, New York, NY 10007.
www.harpercollins.com First Edition 18 19 SCP 30 29 28 27 26 25 24 23

Library of Congress Cataloging in Publication Data. Crews, Donald. Freight Train. "Greenwillow Books."
Summary: Brief text and illustrations trace the journey of a colorful train as it goes through tunnels, by cities, and
over trestles. [1. Railroads—Trains—Pictorial works. 2. Colors. 3. Picture books] I. Title. PZ7.C8682Fr
[E] 78-2303 ISBN 0-688-80165-X (trade) ISBN 0-688-84165-1 (lib. bdg.) ISBN 0-688-11701-5 (pbk.)

Moving.

Going through tunnels

Going by cities

Crossing trestles.

gone.

Moving in daylight.
Going, going...

With due respect to Casey Jones, John Henry, The Rock Island Line,
and the countless freight trains passed and passing the big house in Cottondale

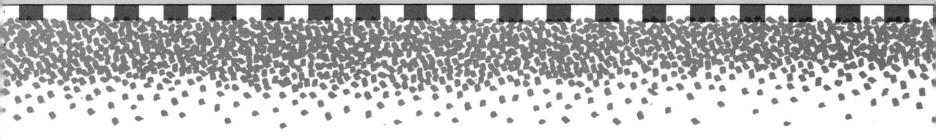

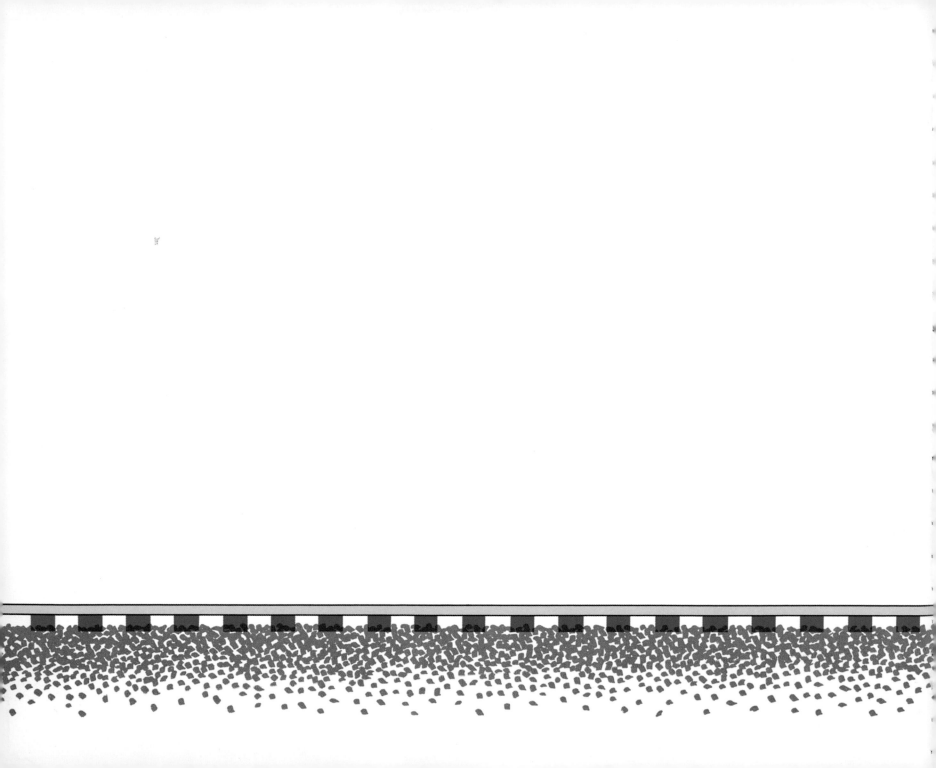

**Red caboose
at the back**

**Orange
tank
car
next**

A train runs across this track.

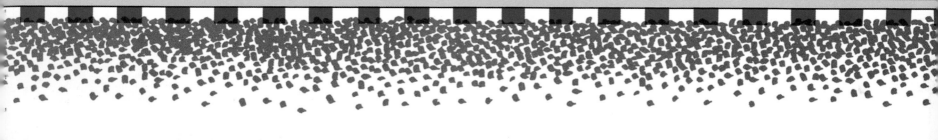

Yellow
hopper car

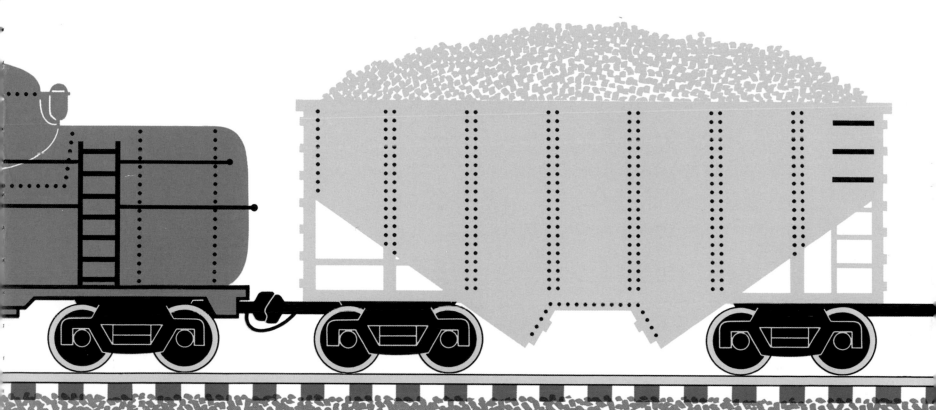

**Green
cattle car**

**Blue
gondola
car**

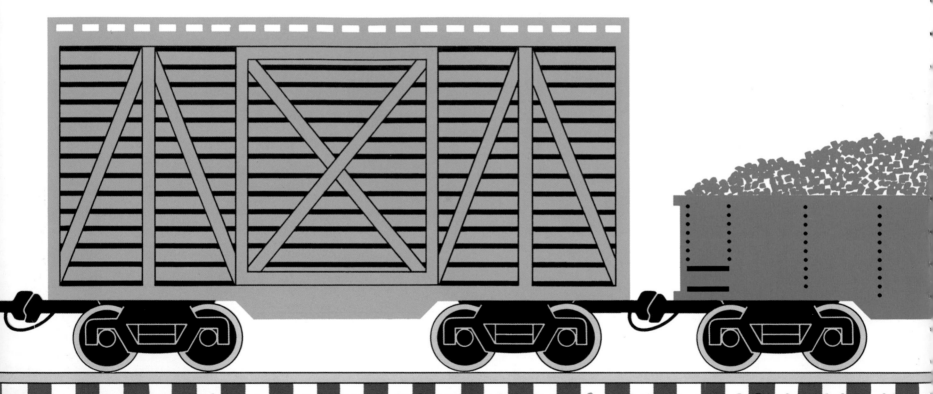

Purple
box car

a Black tender and

a Black
steam engine.

Freight train.